PARTY
SAVERS

by E. S. Mooney
Based on
"THE POWERPUFF GIRLS,"
as created by Craig McCracken

SCHOLASTIC INC.

New York Toronto London Auckland Sydney
Mexico City New Delhi Hong Kong

ISBN 0-439-24326-2

Designed by Peter Koblish

Illustrated by Art Ruiz

12 11 10 9 8 7 6 5   1 2 3 4 5 6/0

Printed in the U.S.A.
First Scholastic printing, April 2001

SUGAR . . .

SPICE . . .

and everything nice . . .

These were the ingredients chosen to

create the perfect little girl.

But Professor Utonium accidentally

added an extra ingredient to

the concoction —

CHEMICAL X!

And thus, The Powerpuff Girls were born!

Using their ultra superpowers,

BLOSSOM,

BUBBLES,

and BUTTERCUP

have dedicated their lives to fighting crime

and the forces of evil!

Chapter 1

The city of Townsville . . .

It's a perfect day for recess at Pokey Oaks Kindergarten. The Powerpuff Girls have been working very hard on their p's and q's. Now it's recess and time for a little fun!

"P-Q-J-G-Y-la-la-la! Bubbles hopped across the hopscotch board, singing.

"What is that song?" Buttercup asked her sister.

"It's my new favorite." Bubbles giggled.

"Well, I've never heard of it," Buttercup snapped.

"Why are you in such a bad mood?" Blossom asked her sister.

"Haven't you noticed anything strange?" Buttercup turned to look at the rest of the playground.

Blossom turned, too. She studied the other kindergartners. They were all chatting about something and seemed very excited.

"What's going on?" Bubbles asked.

"Harry Pit is having a birthday party at Townsville Amusement Park," Buttercup announced.

"Oooohhh!" Bubbles squealed. "That will be so much fun!"

"Yeah," agreed Blossom. "We'll have a great time!"

"No," snapped Butter-
cup. "*They* will have a great
time. *We* are not invited!"

"That's silly," said Blossom.
"Of course we're invited if
everyone else is."

"I want to go." Bubbles's eyes
were starting to fill with tears.

"I was standing right there when he
passed out the invitations!" Buttercup
was almost shouting. "He gave one to
everyone but me!"

Blossom saw her friend Mary nearby
on the swings. "I'll ask Mary. There must
be some mistake. Hey, Mary, come
here!"

Mary turned to The Powerpuff Girls.
She smiled at Blossom and ran over.
"Hi, you guys!" she said.

"Mary, is it true that Harry is having a party, and everyone is invited but us?"

"W-w-well," Mary stammered, "I guess so. But Harry wasn't trying to be mean. He figured you would be bored. After all, you guys are superheroes! You fly around and have adventures every day! Normal kids like us have to go to an amusement park to do that."

The Girls stared at Mary. They didn't say anything.

Mary looked upset. "Harry just thinks you guys are really, really cool. He didn't want you to think his party was stupid," she said quietly.

"We would never think his party was stupid," Bubbles piped up.

"It's okay, Mary," said Blossom sadly. "Thanks for telling us."

Just then, the bell rang. The Girls dragged themselves back into school.

Oh, my. Just look at those sad faces. It's going to be a long afternoon.

Meanwhile, in Townsville Central Park, trouble was brewing at the headquarters of the archenemy of The Powerpuff Girls, Mojo Jojo. . . .

Mojo stood before an army of mean-looking robots. The scary simian paced around the room.

"At last I will be taking over the entire city of Townsville! I have been trying to take over the city ever since those pesky little Powerpuff Girls were born. But now I have a whole army of superpowered destructo-robots. And now nothing can stop me!

"Now . . . NOW . . . finally, I will rule! But I must destroy those Girls first."

Mojo paced the floor. "Now, what is my plan? It must be better than all other plans." He scratched his chin. "I must find the perfect way to surprise them. But how to know exactly where they'll be . . . Hmm . . .

"It's time to do a little undercover work," he decided. "There's only one way to find out what The Powerpuff Girls are up to! Spy on them! I will find out exactly where they'll be and what they'll be doing, and then I'll set up a trap that they'll walk right into!"

Uh-oh! Look out, Girls! There's an angry monkey on your backs!

At Pokey Oaks Kindergarten, the last bell finally rang.

The Girls flew home slowly. They were still sad about Harry's party.

"I like being a superhero. I don't even mind being different most of the time —" said Blossom.

"It's really neat to be able to fly around and blow things up and stuff," Buttercup added.

"But I hate not getting to do stuff with the other kids. I want to go to that party!" Bubbles put in.

"It's bad when you can't hang out with your friends," Blossom agreed.

"Maybe the Professor can help," Bubbles chirped.

"Yeah." Blossom tried to sound cheery. "Maybe he can."

Chapter 2

Meanwhile, Professor Utonium had been working in a hot kitchen all afternoon. Professor Utonium was a brilliant scientist. He had created The Powerpuff Girls in one of his experiments, and now he was like the Girls' dad. He was rushing around, putting the final touches on his surprise for the Girls.

"Girls!" the Professor called out. "I'm in the kitchen."

The Girls sighed. They went into the

kitchen. They looked at the Professor with sad eyes.

"Oh, my," declared the Professor. "You Girls seem a little low! Good thing I have a surprise. Look! Super Creamy Powerpuff Balls!"

The Professor waited for the Girls to squeal and shout with delight. But they were silent. They tried to look excited, but it was no use.

"What happened?" The Professor was a little alarmed. "Bubbles?"

Bubbles opened her mouth to speak. But all that came out was a long, sad wail.

"Buttercup?"

"Stupid!" she said, scowling. "Just plain stupid!"

"Blossom?"

"Well," Blossom said slowly, "all the kindergartners were invited to Harry Pit's birthday party at the amusement park."

"Well, that sounds like fun!" the Professor said. But this only made Bubbles cry louder.

"Except us!" Buttercup growled. "We weren't invited!"

"Because we're too . . . cool!" Bubbles sputtered. "He thought because we're superheroes that we wouldn't have a good time!"

"Basically, Professor, we were left out because we're different, and we feel bad," Blossom added.

"I wanna ride on the carousel and the coaster!" Bubbles sobbed.

The Professor had to figure out how to solve this problem. He scratched his chin. Then, suddenly, he smiled and put his finger in the air. "I've got it!"

"You do?" Bubbles asked softly.

"What?" Blossom asked.

"*We* should have a party!"

The three Girls stared at him, dumbfounded.

"How will that help?" Blossom finally asked.

"Could I get a new dress?" Bubbles asked. "I would love a new dress with pretty butterflies and —"

"I don't get it, " Buttercup interrupted. "How will a party help?"

"We'll invite all the kids from school," he said. "They'll come to the house and see that you Girls aren't really so different after all. You live in a normal house. You watch the same TV shows. You probably have the same toys. So even though you Girls are superheroes, you're also pretty normal kids."

"I think it's a genius idea!" Blossom exclaimed.

"I LOVE parties!" Bubbles squealed with glee.

"Oh, all right," said Buttercup. "But I am NOT wearing a party dress!"

"I am! Oh! I am!" Bubbles cried. "And it's going to be blue with gold ribbons and all kinds of beautiful butterflies with little sparkles —"

"Actually," said Blossom, "why don't we make it a costume party?"

"That's great!" the Professor agreed. "That way nobody has to wear a dress . . . unless they want to," he added, smiling at Bubbles.

"I know!" cried Buttercup. "Let's make it a *Come as the Villain You'd Most Like to Beat Up Party!*"

"Can I be a villain with butterflies?" Bubbles asked.

"You can be any kind of villain you want, Bubbles," the Professor said. "Now when is Harry's party?"

"It's two weeks away," Blossom answered.

"Then we'll have our party this Saturday," the Professor announced. "That way, Harry will have time to change his mind and invite you Girls to his party."

"Let's go make the invitations!" Bubbles said.

"Wait!" Buttercup said. "I'm starving!"

Suddenly, the Girls remembered their favorite snack was waiting. They dove for the plate of cream puffs.

Little did the Girls know that Mojo Jojo was standing outside the house. He held a high-powered stethoscope against the kitchen wall.

"Thank you, Powerpuff Girls!" he said with a laugh. "I couldn't have come up with a better plan if I'd come up with it myself!"

Oh, no! What could that simian scoundrel be planning now?

Chapter 3

The next day, at the Pokey Oaks playground . . .

"Hey, Mary!" Blossom shouted.

Mary ran up to her friend. "Yeah, Blossom, what is it?"

"We're having a costume party this Saturday. Will you come?"

"A party at your house? Cool! I can't wait to see where you live!"

Blossom smiled. "It probably looks just like your house," she said.

"Really? Well, okay." Mary looked at the monster on the invitation.

"It's a 'Come as the Villain You'd Most Like to Beat Up Party!'" Buttercup said.

"That's so cool!" Mary exclaimed. "Hey, everybody!" she shouted to the other kids. "Look what The Powerpuff Girls are doing!"

Word spread quickly about the party. Instantly, all the Girls' classmates wanted an invitation.

Just then, the hotline rang. The Girls zipped to the phone.

"Yes, Mayor?" Blossom said.

"We need your help, Girls. Those no-goodnik Gangreen Gangsters are tying up traffic all over town!" the Mayor's voice squawked.

"We'll be right there, Mayor." Blossom hung up the phone. "Downtown, Girls! It's a Gangreen Gridlock Alert!"

Wow! Would you look at that traffic jam! This is definitely more than a case of too many cars and not enough road!

"There they are," Buttercup announced, pointing. The Gangreen Gang was visible in Townsville Town Square. The Girls flew over.

"But what are they doing?" Bubbles asked.

"Looks like they're directing traffic," Blossom said. "And of course, they're doing it all wrong!"

"It's chaos, man! I love it!" The Girls could hear Ace saying to Snake. They were standing at the control panel for the stoplight at the main intersection in town, turning all the lights on and off.

Little Arturo was dressed in a policeman's

uniform. He stood in the middle of the intersection, signaling cars to drive right into one another.

"Excellent, Arturo! Keep up the good work!" Ace shouted.

"Great idea, boss," Big Billy slobbered. "This is really funny!"

Ace laughed. "Another few minutes and we'll have traffic completely stopped. Then we'll be able to rob every store in town. The police won't be able to get to us — so they won't be able to stop us!"

Big Billy clapped his hands and laughed. "Right! They won't be able to stop us." Then the oversized gangster stopped laughing and looked at Ace. "Duh . . . why, boss?"

"Because they'll be stuck in traffic, you idiot!" Ace snapped.

Blossom looked at Ace and Billy and shook her head. "Divide and conquer, Girls!" she shouted.

The Girls swooped into action.

Bubbles slammed into Little Arturo. She grabbed him by the collar and zoomed back into the air.

Buttercup shot an electro-blast at the control box for the streetlights. Grubber and Snake didn't know what hit them. Electricity shot out of the box and straight up their arms.

Blossom went for Ace and Big Billy. She aimed her eye beams right at them. It was all they could take. They both crumpled to the ground.

"Time for cleanup, Girls!" Blossom ordered.

The Girls piled the Gangreen Gang into some garbage cans. Together, they lifted Big Billy up off the ground. They dropped the big, dumb bad guy on top of his gang.

As the citizens of Townsville cheered, the Girls leaped into the air and headed back to school.

"I hate them," Ace mumbled. "It's time to get those kindergartners, once and for all!" He stood up and tried to look tough. He turned to his gang. "Get up!" he shouted. "We're going to see the master-mind himself!"

"Open up!" Ace shouted. He pounded on Mojo's door. Ace was about to pound again when the door swung open. Mojo Jojo stood before them.

"We're the Gangreen Gang," Ace said, trying to sound important.

"I know who you are," Mojo bellowed. "You're the idiots who give villains and monsters a bad name. Why is it that you are bothering me when everyone knows I do not like to be bothered?"

"Uhhh . . ." Ace said nervously. He was a little afraid of Mojo.

"We wanna get The Powerpuff Girls —
once and for all," Big Billy announced.
"Duh . . . right, boss?"

"Right," Ace agreed. "We want to join
forces to crush them."

"I see," said Mojo slowly. "Well . . . it is
most timely that you should be knocking
on my door in the way that you are knocking. The time has come to bring those tiny
titans to their knees! Do come in."

Later that evening . . .

"Okay, we'll split up," said Ace. "Big
Billy and Grubber, come with me. We'll
deliver this invitation to Fuzzy. The rest of
you — take this one."

Ace handed Snake an envelope. When
Snake and Little Arturo saw the name on
the envelope, they gasped. It said, HIM.

"We'll meet back here in an hour to pass out the rest," Ace interrupted.

"But —" said Little Arturo.

"Look," barked Ace, "these are orders from Mojo! Now let's go!" Ace turned and took off. Snake sighed, and he and Arturo headed in the other direction.

Oh, no! Girls, there's real trouble brewing now! Mojo is inviting every villain in town to your party! Help! Somebody stop the madness!

Chapter 4

The next evening in The Powerpuff Girls' bed-room . . . Hey! What's going on? Why are there three villains in their room? And why are they laughing and pointing at one an-other? Oh . . . never mind . . . I get it. . . .

"I can't stand it!" Bubbles said, laughing.

"You look totally monstrous!" Blossom cried.

Buttercup's head popped up. She crawled out of her Big Billy costume. She started laughing, too.

Blossom pulled off a bucket she was using as a helmet. She was almost done with her Mojo head.

"I'm a beautiful, ugly hillbilly monster!" sang Bubbles. She was dressed up like Fuzzy Lumpkins. But her overalls were embroidered with butterflies.

"I have to make my arms longer," said Blossom. "I want them to drag on the floor!"

"He's so ugly," Bubbles said. "Why did you pick Mojo?"

"He may be ugly, but he's smart," said Blossom. "And I'm more interested in brains than beauty!"

27

The Girls went back to work. Their costumes had to be perfect. It was going to be the best party ever.

"Girls?" the Professor called. "Will you come down here? I need your help."

The Girls zipped downstairs.

"At your service, Professor." Buttercup giggled.

"Well, you Girls are certainly in a good mood," said the Professor.

"We just want to thank you, Professor," Bubbles said. "This party is the funnest thing in the whole world."

"Well, that's actually why I called you. I've been working all day on party favors for your guests."

The Girls jumped up and down.

"But I'm not sure which of my creations would be the best. Could I demonstrate them for you? Then you could tell me what you think."

"Shoot!" said Blossom. "Show us what you've got!"

"Well, I thought it might be fun to give your friends a superpower of their own. That way they'll really feel like you've all got something in common!"

The Girls looked surprised. It sounded a bit dangerous.

"Are you sure, Professor?" Blossom asked.

"Oh, they're only temporary, Girls. Just powerful enough to last for the party."

"What are they?" asked Buttercup.

"This is the Personal High-Flying Power Pack," he announced.

He strapped himself into a machine that looked like a backpack. "You just push this button—"

KABLAM!

In an instant, the Professor had disappeared! The Girls coughed.

"Professor!" Bubbles sounded frightened. "Where are you?"

"Up here, Girls."

The Girls looked up at the ceiling. The Professor was stuck to it.

"I guess I haven't quite perfected this one," he said sheepishly.

"Yeah," Blossom agreed. "That one might be a little too powerful."

"Okay. Well, the second choice is this," he said. He put on a pair of glasses made from huge marble balls. "Eye Beam Balls! You just put them on, and when you blink — "

ZZZZAAAAPPPPP!

A big round hole suddenly appeared in the living room wall. The Girls stared in amazement. They could see right through the wall.

"Uh, Professor?" Buttercup said.

"Right. Guess that's not quite ready, either."

"I think we need to lock up these toys," Blossom said, worried.

"I'm sure this one will work," the Professor announced. "Supersticky Silly String! Spray it on any two things and they will stick together like cement!"

The Professor shot a line of string right at a chair. Then he fired it at a lamp. In an instant, the chair and lamp slammed together.

"Wow!" said Buttercup. "Cool!"

Bubbles and Blossom tried to pry apart the lamp and chair, but it was impossible.

"This seems like it could cause trouble," Blossom said. "Couldn't kids get stuck together?"

"It only lasts for about twenty minutes," the Professor assured them. "Just long enough for a good laugh. Then it evaporates."

"Let's give them the string," Buttercup said.

"Yeah, the string!" Bubbles agreed.

"Okay," said Blossom. "But if the entire kindergarten class shows up as one big blob on Monday morning, don't say I didn't warn you!"

Meanwhile, at Mojo's volcano top observatory . . . the phone was ringing.

"To whom am I speaking?" Mojo asked.

"It is I." It was a voice so eerie it made even an evil monkey nervous.

"Ah! You received your invitation to the party?" Mojo breathed.

"Indeed. I am calling to respond." The scary voice chuckled. "I will be delighted to attend!"

Oh, no! It's Him! Beware, Girls, beware!

Chapter 5

The night of the party . . .

The Powerpuff Girls were in the living room, putting the final adjustments on their costumes. They giggled as they admired one another's outfits.

"It's almost time, Girls!" The Professor stepped out of the kitchen. He was wearing a long white apron and a big poofy hat. "Cookies?" he asked. He whipped out a tray from the kitchen.

34

"Yeah!" the Girls shouted.

Just then, the doorbell rang.

The Girls raced to the door. The moment it opened, a flood of monsters poured into the room. There were three Fuzzys, five Mojos, and at least two of each member of the Gangreen Gang.

"Hey, Bubbles!"

"Hi, Blossom!"

"Great costume, Buttercup!"

With everyone wearing costumes, it was hard to tell who was talking.

"Wow!" whispered Blossom.

"This is a lot of kids!" responded Buttercup.

"Maybe all the kids in our class thought our party was going to be so cool they brought a friend," Blossom said.

"What about the party favors? The Professor only made enough for our class!" Bubbles looked worried. "With all these costumes, we don't even know who's in our class and who isn't."

"Good point," answered Buttercup. "Boy, some of these costumes are re-e-a-a-lly good!"

"I know it sounds mean," Blossom said slowly, "but since the Professor made just enough — we should only pass them out to our classmates. If only we knew how to tell them apart."

"We'll just peek under their masks," Bubbles suggested. "If they're in our class, then they get a party favor. If they're not, we'll just say hello and welcome."

"Okay. That sounds like a good plan," Blossom said.

The party was an instant success. The music was blasting and the kids were gobbling up the Professor's cakes and cookies. Bubbles stood next to the cookie tray and waited for kids to lift up their masks to eat. If she knew them, she gave them a can of Supersticky Silly String.

Blossom and Buttercup were showing some of the kids their books and toys.

"I have that game!" said someone in an Ace costume. Blossom recognized the voice. It was her friend Mary.

"It's my favorite," Blossom said.

"Mine, too!" Mary squealed.

"Have a party favor!" Blossom handed Mary a can of string.

"Great party favors!" Harry Pit said as he dashed out of the room. He looked like a very small Fuzzy. "I'm gonna go downstairs and stick some stuff together!"

At the food table, Bubbles handed Elmer Sglue a party favor. "Just don't eat it, Elmer," she whispered.

Elmer was dressed up like Little Arturo. "Wow!" he cried. "Cool!" He grabbed the can of string. Before Bubbles knew what was happening, the cake was stuck to the chandelier.

"Maybe you should play with it out-doors," Blossom said.

"I am a superhero!" Elmer shouted. "I challenge you all!"

The kids laughed.

"It's going really well," Blossom whispered to Buttercup.

"I know!" Buttercup agreed. "Everyone's hav-ing a great time!"

At that very moment, Bubbles let out a shout. "It doesn't come off!"

"What's wrong?" Buttercup yelled across the room. Bubbles was standing next to a kid dressed up as Mojo.

"It's not a costume!" Bubbles shouted.

Blossom leaped into the air and zipped

over to her sister. "What are you talking about?"

"Look!" Bubbles said. She tugged on the face of the Mojo that stood in front of her. The mask didn't move.

Blossom stared through her own Mojo mask. Then, the other Mojo spoke.

"If I were easily offended I would be very offended by that ridiculous costume you are wearing, which is supposed to look like me! My arms are NOT that long!"

All the kids had gone quiet. They were watching the two Mojos.

It took Blossom a minute to realize what was happening. She was in a Mojo Jojo face-off — and the other Mojo was for real!

chapter 6

All the kids started screaming. They tried to get away from Mojo. But then the other villains started to attack. The kids screamed even louder. They ran back and forth through the living room and dining room, trying to hide.

"Oh, no!" shouted Buttercup. "There are REAL villains all over the place!"

Bubbles was furious. "How dare they ruin our party!" she shrieked.

Blossom knew they had to act fast. "Girls!" she shouted. Her sisters zoomed up to her. "We've got to stop this, quick! Before someone gets hurt."

"I'll take Fuzzy," Bubbles announced.

"I'll take the Gangreen Gang," Buttercup said. "But that's not the real problem. How are we going to tell the real villains from our friends?"

The Girls looked down at the living room. Monsters and villains were everywhere! They were all running around, and it was impossible to tell who was chasing whom.

"We gotta get the kids to take off their masks," Blossom declared.

"If you are wearing a mask, take it off!" Bubbles screeched.

It took a minute for the party-goers to recover from Bubbles's supersonic scream.

42

But then, all the kids ripped off their masks. At last, it was clear who the real bad guys were.

"Okay, Powerpuff Girls!" Blossom announced. "Let's do it!"

Blossom dove right at Mojo. But he had his gigantic laser blaster and lots of other nasty toys. Blossom was having a tough time battling him.

But Buttercup couldn't help her. She was busy trying to beat up all five Gangreen Gangsters at once.

Bubbles, however, was really mad about their party being ruined. It gave her extra energy to battle Fuzzy. The notorious hillbilly criminal was in serious trouble.

Blossom was
just about to
shoot an eye
beam when a group
of kids ran through
her line of fire. She
stopped herself so the kids wouldn't get
hurt. That gave Mojo time to blast her.

"Blossom!" shouted Bubbles. She
rushed to her sister. Blossom was out
cold.

"Okay, you monkey-meanie! I'll take
care of you!" Bubbles shot into the air and
aimed straight for Mojo. But the monkey
dodged the blow.

"I could use a little help!" Buttercup
shouted. The Gangreen Gang had her
backed into a corner. Blossom pulled
herself up from the floor. She zoomed

over to help Buttercup. But a new round of screaming stopped her.

She turned around to see Mojo aiming his blaster at a group of kids huddled in a corner.

"This time you will not beat us, Powerpuff Girls!" Mojo announced.

"Stop!" shouted Blossom. "Leave the other kids alone!" Blossom was starting to worry that they couldn't beat all these villains at once. All their friends were in the way.

Just then, the Professor came out from the kitchen. He had no idea what was happening.

"Watch out!" Buttercup shouted.

Mojo had sent a superpowerful blast right at the Professor.

"Ugh!" The Professor was dazed. His

eyes spun in circles. "I thought the party had gotten a little loud," he sputtered. Then, he fell over.

Oh, no! Is this the end of The Powerpuff Girls? And what about all the rest of those cute little kindergartners? Oh, my, oh, my . . . what will Townsville do with no kindergartners?

chapter 7

"How dare you!" Buttercup shouted in rage. "How dare you attack the Professor!" She shot through the air, straight at Mojo. He aimed his blaster at her.

"Buttercup!" Blossom grabbed her sister in midair and knocked her out of the way of the blast. Buttercup and Blossom flew toward the ceiling. Bubbles joined them.

"We've got to think this through, Girls!" Blossom said urgently.

"They're using our friends as hostages!" Buttercup growled. "And they attacked the Professor!"

"All this is happening because we wanted to be like our friends," Bubbles said, shaking her head. "If only our friends were more like us. Then they could save themselves!"

Blossom looked at Bubbles and smiled. "Exactly! Great idea, Bubbles! I'm going to talk to the kids. You two, cover me!"

Blossom zipped down to their friends. "Attention, all Pokey Oakers!"

All the kids gathered around in a huddle. Bubbles and Buttercup defended the group from attacks.

"We need your help!" Blossom told her friends. "We can beat these guys if we all use our superpowers together!"

The kids looked confused.

"What superpowers?" Mary asked.

"You all got party favors, right?" Blossom answered.

The kids nodded excitedly.

"One can of Supersticky Silly String isn't that powerful," Blossom continued. "But if you all use them together —"

The kids started to smile and nod.

"Get your party favors!" Blossom commanded.

The kids scrambled for their cans of string.

"Are we gonna stick it to 'em?" Bubbles squeaked.

"That's the plan!" Blossom announced.

Blossom zoomed down to Mary and whispered in her ear. Mary nodded and quickly whispered to Elmer. Elmer nodded and whispered to one of the kids who was standing near him. In no time the kindergartners were all whispering.

Meanwhile, Fuzzy was making a lot of noise over in the corner. He had grabbed a chandelier and started swinging from it.

"Bubbles and Buttercup! Eye beams on Fuzzy!" Blossom commanded.

Bubbles and Buttercup turned to Fuzzy and

shot a double-trouble eye beam straight at him. The kids surrounded Fuzzy. Blossom shouted, "NOW!"

The kids all aimed their Super String at Fuzzy. Instantly, he was covered in sticky gooey string. Then they all aimed their string at the wall. Before Fuzzy could blink, he was slammed against the wall. He was stuck! The kids let out a cheer.

"Okay, kids! Attention!" Blossom shouted.

Just then, Mojo sent a blast straight at the Girls. Blossom and Bubbles darted away, but Buttercup didn't see it coming. She fell to the floor. Elmer ran to her.

"Buttercup!" he shouted. But she didn't answer.

Bubbles flew over to her sister. "You stay with Buttercup, Elmer. Everyone else, come on!"

Bubbles and Blossom flew into action. The Girls dove at the Gangreen Gang. The kindergartners started surrounding them. Blossom and Bubbles flew faster and faster in a circle around the gang. They were making the gang dizzy. Soon, they were backed up against one another.

Blossom shouted, "NOW!"

The kindergartners plastered the gang with their Super String. The gang stuck to one another in every way. Ace's arm was stuck to Little Arturo's leg. Snake was upside down with his head stuck to Big Billy's foot. Grubber was stuck sideways across Big Billy's belly.

Bubbles couldn't help giggling. They looked so funny.

Off in the corner, Him had stopped giggling. Things were not going according to his plan.

"Well, I certainly enjoyed myself," Him said. "Thank you so much for having me. Hate to destroy and run . . . but I really must go!" Then he melted into thin air.

Mojo was on his own. He aimed his blaster at Bubbles. She went tumbling. Buttercup was starting to rally. But it was up to Blossom to battle the monkey all by herself. It was a showdown: Mojo vs. Mojo!

Blossom gathered all her superstrength and opened her mouth wide. She blew out ice as hard as she could.

Before he could move a muscle, Mojo was frozen solid.

Suddenly, it was quiet. The kids looked around as if they were waiting for the next attack. But one by one, they realized they had beaten all the bad guys! As Buttercup and Bubbles opened their eyes, they looked as amazed as their friends.

"Wow!" exclaimed Mary. "Saving the day is *cool*!"

"You're all superheroes!" announced Blossom.

The Pokey Oaks superheroes let out a huge cheer. The Powerpuff Girls lifted the frozen and sticky villains and flew them out to the curb.

"Good thing it's trash day!" shouted Buttercup.

Finally, the Girls were ready to cele-

brate. After all, it was still a party! But then another strange noise was heard.

"Uugghh . . . uuuhhhh . . . aagghh!" It was the Professor!

"Oh, no!" cried Buttercup. "We forgot about the Professor!"

What's wrong with the Professor? Oh, no! And just when it looked like there would be a happy ending!

Chapter 8

"Professor!" shouted Blossom. "Can you hear me?"

The Professor looked at Blossom with a blank stare. Then he looked at a tray of cookies nearby. He lifted up the platter and held it out.

"Cookies, anyone?" he asked.

The kids stared in surprised silence. Then everybody laughed. The kids dove for the platter. They gobbled up the cookies and all started gabbing at once about their big victory.

The Girls flew over to the Professor.

"You're the best!" Blossom said. She hugged the Professor.

"We're the luckiest little girls in the world," Bubbles squeaked. She kissed the Professor on the cheek.

Buttercup grabbed a cookie. "Awesome cookies, Professor."

Just then, Harry Pit walked up to the Girls. "Wow," he said. "This is definitely the most exciting party I've ever been to. You Girls really know how to have fun!" Harry looked at the floor. He seemed suddenly shy. "I know it's a little last-minute — but I was hoping — well, *really* hoping — would you PLEASE come to my party?"

The Girls smiled.

"It just won't be a party if you're not there," Harry said.

"We'd love to come," squealed Bubbles.

All the kids cheered.

"I think the party was a pretty big success," the Professor said. He looked around the room at all the cheering kids. But then he frowned.

"What's wrong, Professor?" Buttercup asked.

"It's just too bad that the kids never got to use their party favors."

The Girls looked at one another and giggled.

"I guess you missed a little bit of the action," Blossom said. "Don't worry, Professor. Your party favors tied things up nicely."

And so, once again, the day is saved, thanks to The Powerpuff Girls. And let's not forget their friends and, of course, the Professor. Now there's a man who really understands the importance of STICKING TOGETHER!